Sherlock Bones Looks at Physical Science

Sound

Harriet McGregor

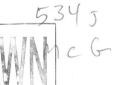

WINDMILL
BOOKS
New York

Published in 2011 by Windmill Books, LLC
303 Park Avenue South, Suite #1280, New York, NY 10010-3657

First Edition

Senior Editor: Camilla Lloyd
Designer: Simon Borrough
Consultant: Jon Turney
Picture Researcher: Amy Sparks
Illustrator: Stefan Chabluk
Sherlock Bones Artwork: Richard Hook

Photographs:
Abbreviations: t-top, b-bottom, l-left, r-right, m-middle.
Cover: Istockphoto (John Stelzer); **Insides: Folios** Dreamstime (Starush); **1**
Shutterstock (Alexandru Chiriac); **4** Photolibrary (Stefean Auth); **5** Dreamstime (Leo
Bruce); **6** Dreamstime (Starush); **9** Shutterstock (Zsolt, Biczó); **10** (l) Dreamstime
(Tzooka), (r) Dreamstime (Addyts); **11** (tr) Dreamstime (Elaine Nash), (bl) Dreamstime
(Robert Plotz); **12** Dreamstime (Brad Calkins); **13** NASA; **14** Dreamstime (Keeweeboy);
15 Dreamstime (Pressmaster); **16** (l) Dreamstime (Fibobejcts), (c) Shutterstock
(Nicholas Sutcliffe), (r) Dreamstime (Kolyzh); **17** Istockphoto (John Stelzer); **18**
Istockphoto (Bart Coenders); **23** Shutterstock (Sergey Popov); **24** Shutterstock
(Alexandru Chiriac); **25** Shutterstock (Norma Cornes); **26** Shutterstock (Mikael
Damkier); **27** Shutterstock (tstockphoto).

Library of Congress Cataloging-in-Publication Data

McGregor, Harriet.
 Sound / by Harriet McGregor. — 1st ed.
    p. cm. — (Sherlock Bones looks at physical science)
 Includes index.
 ISBN 978-1-61533-215-1 (library binding)
 1. Sound—Juvenile literature. I. Title.
 QC225.5.M42 2011
 534—dc22
                          2010024567

Manufactured in China

For more great fiction and nonfiction, go to www.windmillbooks.com

CPSIA Compliance Information: Batch #WAW1102W: For Further Information contact Windmill Books, New York, New York on 1-866-478-0556.

Contents

Words that appear in **bold** can be found in the glossary on page 30.

The Science Detective, Sherlock Bones, will help you learn all about Sound. The answers to Sherlock's questions can be found on page 31.

What Is Sound?

Sound is a part of everyday life. Your footsteps on a carpet make a quiet sound. Slamming a door shut as you leave your home makes a loud sound. You **communicate** using sound as you talk to your friends.

Vibrations

Sounds are made when objects **vibrate**. A vibration is when something moves back and forth very rapidly. Place your hand on the front of your neck and speak or sing. You can feel the vibrations as you make a sound. A tuning fork struck on a table vibrates and makes a ringing sound. If the tuning fork is placed in water, the vibrations splash the water.

🐾 **In what other situations can you feel sound's vibrations?**

▼ **This large drum vibrates when it is struck.**

Sound Energy

Sound is a type of **energy**. Other types of energy can be turned into sound energy. In a stereo system, electrical energy turns into sound energy. In a washing machine, electrical energy turns into movement energy and sound energy.

▶ **Imagine walking along this busy street. What sounds would you hear?**

THE SCIENCE DETECTIVE INVESTIGATES:

See Sound's Energy

You will need:
• stereo system • CD • feather

1 Put the CD in the stereo system and check that it can play music loudly.
2 Turn the sound on the stereo system down low.
3 Hold the feather close to the speaker and gradually turn up the volume of the music. Watch the feather and the speaker. What happens?

As the music gets louder, the feather starts to move. You might also see the stereo speaker move. The vibrations of the speaker create sound energy. The sound energy travels through the air and moves the feather.

How Does Sound Travel?

Sound travels as waves. You hear sound when **sound waves** travel through the air to your ears. The closer you are to a sound, the more clearly you hear it. A firework display up close can be extremely loud, but from a distance, fireworks sound much quieter.

◀ Fireworks make very loud sounds. The vibrations travel through the air as sound waves.

SCIENCE AT WORK

If you screamed in space, another human could not hear you. There are not enough particles to carry the sound to their ears.

Passing on Energy

All substances are made up of tiny particles. When a bat hits a ball, it vibrates and creates sound. The bat's vibration makes the air particles around it vibrate also. The air particles bump into each other and pass on the vibration. In this way, sound waves travel through the air away from the bat.

Solids, Liquids, and Gases

Sound travels better through solids and liquids than it does through air (gas). The particles that make up solids and liquids are closer together than the particles that make up air. It is therefore easier for the particles to bump into each other and pass on the sound waves.

In air, sound travels at 1,125 ft./sec. (343 m/sec.). In sea water, sound travels at 5,030 ft./sec. (1,533 m/sec.). In solid iron, sound travels 16,830 ft./sec. (5,130 m/sec.).

THE SCIENCE DETECTIVE INVESTIGATES:

Bumping Molecules

You will need:
• tape • 6 ball bearings or marbles • string (cut into six 4-in. (10-cm) lengths) • coat hanger

1 Use tape to stick a ball bearing to the end of each piece of string.
2 Tie each string to the coat hanger as shown in the diagram. Hook the coat hanger to a shower rail or curtain pole and check that it hangs level.
3 Pull back the first ball bearing and release it so that it hits the next one. What happens?

The ball bearings hit one another in turn, passing on their energy (see below). This is how sound travels.

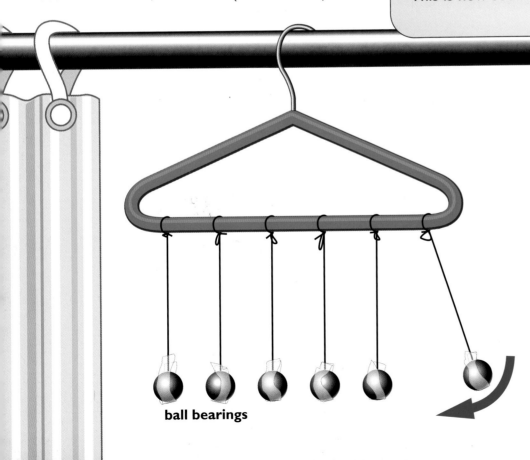

ball bearings

How Do Humans Hear?

S it still in a quiet room and listen. Even when your surroundings are quiet, there are usually sounds to hear. You might hear your own breathing, cars driving past outside, birds singing, or a clock ticking. The human ear is perfectly shaped to catch even the quietest of sounds.

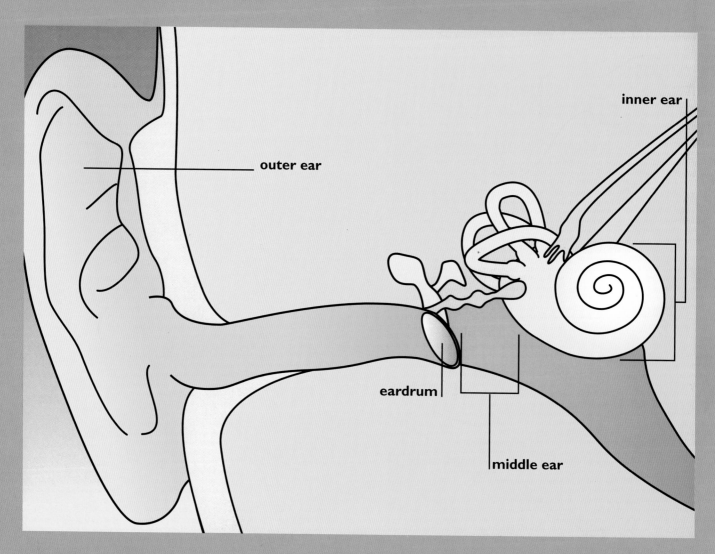

outer ear

inner ear

eardrum

middle ear

Human Ears

When you listen to a radio, the sound waves travel from the radio to your ear. Your outer ear channels the waves inside to your **eardrum**. The eardrum is a very thin sheet of skin. The sound vibrations move the eardrum back and forth. The eardrum passes this movement on to tiny bones in the middle ear. The movement of the bones causes fluid and tiny hairs to move inside the inner ear. The inner ear sends signals to the brain. The brain understands these signals as sound and you hear the radio.

▲ Sound waves are collected by the outer ear and channeled through the middle ear, to the inner ear.

🐾 How could you use your hands to help your ears catch more sounds?

Direction of Sound

If you close your eyes and listen, you can probably tell which direction a sound is coming from. This is because you have two ears. If an object to your left makes a sound, the sound arrives at your left ear sooner than your right ear. Your brain can detect this difference and tell you which direction the sound has come from.

◀ **When you listen carefully, it is possible to tell from which direction a car is coming. You can do this because you have two ears.**

THE SCIENCE DETECTIVE INVESTIGATES:

Catching Sounds

place your ear here

place this end on your friend's chest

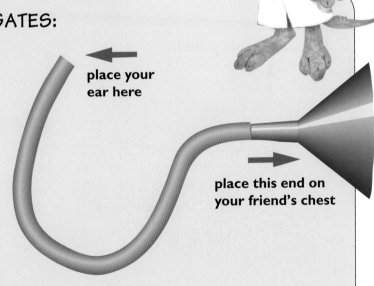

You will need:
• funnel • rubber tube • scissors

Make a device to catch quiet sounds and channel them to your ear.

1 Push a small funnel into one end of a rubber tube. If you need to make the funnel opening larger, cut it an inch or so from the small end.
2 Hold the funnel to the left side of someone's chest or to a ticking watch.
3 Put the tube end to your ear. What can you hear? How does it work?

The wide funnel collects lots of sound waves and channels them down the tube to your ear. This makes sounds that are normally too quiet to hear seem louder.

How Do Other Animals Hear?

Animal ears come in all shapes and sizes. Elephants have huge, flapping ears, foxes have pointed ears, and a seal's ears are very hard to see. Some animals have excellent hearing. If you have ever taken a dog for a walk, you may have noticed it suddenly prick its ears and look alert. Dogs can hear sounds that we can't hear.

Animal Ears

An animal's ears are perfectly suited to its lifestyle. Rabbits have long ears that can turn in the direction of sound. This helps them to locate danger and keep safe. Elephant ears not only allow them to hear, but they also keep the elephant cool. A bird does not have outer ears, but their inner ears are similar to those of a human. By not having outer ears, the bird keeps its **streamlined** shape, which helps it fly smoothly through the air.

▲ This rabbit is alert, listening for signs of danger.

◀ The fennec fox lives in North Africa. It has huge ears to catch sound and keep cool. It loses lots of heat from its ears.

Animal Sounds

Sound travels faster and farther through water than through air. This allows whales to communicate over vast distances. Whale song is loud and low, and can cross oceans more than 1,553 miles (2,500 km) wide. Insects such as crickets and cicadas also communicate using sound. Male crickets chirp by rubbing their wings together. They do this to attract females and to scare away other males. Crickets hear through ears located just below the knees of their front legs.

▲ Barn owls use their excellent hearing to find prey such as mice, voles, and rats.

▲ Whales, such as this humpback whale, make moans, howls, and cries that can continue for hours.

SCIENCE AT WORK

Owls are excellent hunters and can locate **prey** in complete darkness. Barn owls' faces are shaped like concave (curved inwards) discs. This shape channels sound waves to their ears. One ear is usually higher than the other, which allows the owl to tell the exact direction from which a sound is coming.

Are Sounds All the Same?

Sounds can be high, low, loud, and quiet. Get up and walk around the room. What sounds do you make? Your clothes might rustle softly as you move, your feet might thud loudly on the floor, or the floorboards might squeak. The sounds are different because the objects are made of different materials and vibrate in different ways.

Pitch

The **pitch** of a sound means how high or low it is. High-pitched sounds include the squeak of a mouse, the cry of a baby, and the top note of a xylophone. When objects vibrate quickly, they make a high-pitched sound. Low-pitched sounds include the rumble of thunder, a knock at the front door, and the voice of a large man. When objects vibrate slowly, they make a low-pitched sound.

🐾 **Which of the following sounds has a high pitch? A bird singing, a car engine, a lawn mower, a child talking, an adult talking.**

SCIENCE AT WORK

Scientists believe that around 65 million years ago, an **asteroid** fell to Earth and killed off the dinosaurs. The sound of the asteroid crashing is thought to be the loudest sound ever heard on Earth. In more recent times, one of the loudest sounds was the eruption of the Krakatau volcano in Indonesia in 1883. The sound was so loud that it was heard more than 3,000 miles (4,830 km) away. The **shock wave** is said to have circled the Earth several times.

▼ **Chicks make high-pitched cheeping sounds to tell their parents that they are hungry.**

Loudness

The more energy there is in a sound wave, the louder it is. Slamming a door shut makes a loud sound. The vibrations are large and the sound waves have lots of energy. Gently tapping a pencil on a table makes a quiet sound. The vibrations are small and the sound waves have less energy.

◀ **A rocket blasting off into space makes an extremely loud sound.**

How Do We Make Sounds with our Voices?

Singing, talking, shouting, crying, screaming, and whispering are all ways of making sounds with our voices. We can make high sounds, low sounds, loud sounds, and quiet sounds. We can use our mouths and tongues to shape sounds into words. We can communicate our **emotions** with our voices.

Making Sound

You breathe air in and out of your lungs. Your larynx (voice box) is in your windpipe. Inside the larynx are two very thin membranes called the **vocal cords**. When you breathe in and out, air passes over the vocal cords. The vocal cords vibrate and create a sound.

▼ **Singers practice regularly to exercise their vocal cords and keep their voice sounding its best.**

SCIENCE AT WORK

It is possible, but very difficult, for a human to make a glass shatter using their voice. When an object is struck, it naturally vibrates at a particular **note**. Tapping a crystal wine glass makes it vibrate with a clear note sound. If an opera singer is able to sing loudly enough at that exact note, it makes the glass vibrate more and more. Eventually, if the singer's voice is powerful and accurate enough, the glass shatters.

High, Low, Loud, and Soft

The vocal cords tighten and move closer together to make a high-pitched sound. They relax and move apart to make a low-pitched sound. Men have larger vocal cords than women and children. This makes mens' voices lower pitched.

To shout loudly, you force air out of your body quickly and forcibly over your vocal cords. To talk softly, you force air out more slowly and gently.

One of a Kind

Your speaking and singing voice is unique (one of a kind). How you sound depends on the size and shape of your vocal cords and the rest of your body. In particular, the shape of your chest and neck, your overall size and bone structure, and the position of your tongue all affect how your voice sounds.

🐾 **Are your vocal cords close together or further apart when you make a high-pitched scream?**

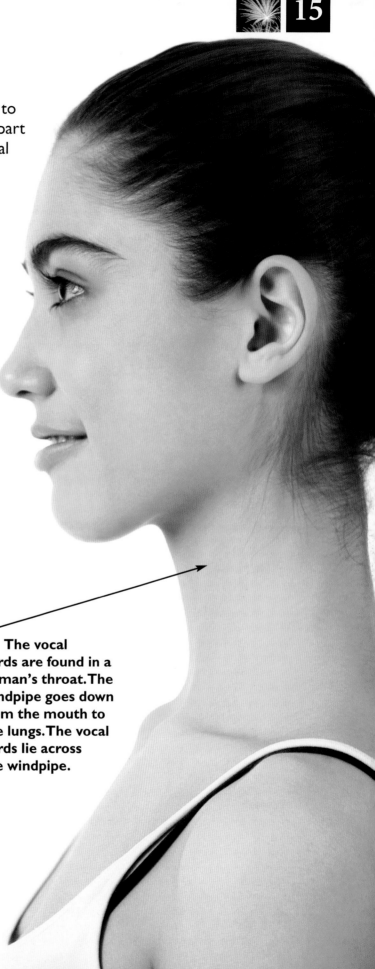

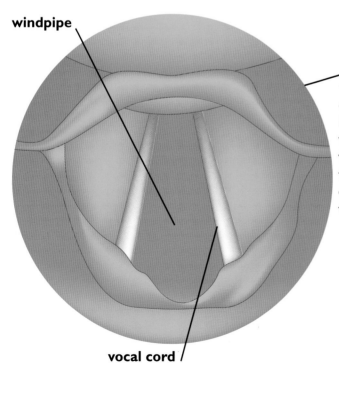

windpipe

vocal cord

◀ **The vocal cords are found in a human's throat. The windpipe goes down from the mouth to the lungs. The vocal cords lie across the windpipe.**

What Is Music?

Music is the arrangement of notes in a way that sounds pleasant. There are a huge variety of music types. You may have a favorite style of music or particular bands that you enjoy listening to. Keyboard, string, wind, **percussion**, and electronic are all types of musical instrument.

String Instruments

Violins, guitars, and cellos are string instruments. When the strings are plucked, strummed, or played with a bow, they vibrate and make a sound. The vibrations are **amplified** (made louder) by the hollow body of the instrument, or by an electronic amplifier. Each string has a different thickness. Thin strings vibrate quickly and make a high-pitched sound. Thick strings vibrate more slowly and make a low-pitched sound.

◀ The body of a violin (right) is approximately 14 in. (35 cm) long. A cello's body (left) is about 30 in. (76 cm) long. The violin has shorter, thinner strings that make higher-pitched sounds than the cello.

▼ These musicians are playing their string instruments in a string quartet.

Wind Instruments

Flutes, clarinets, and recorders are wind instruments. To make a wind instrument work, you blow in or across an opening. The column of air inside the instrument vibrates and makes a sound. Recorders have holes that you cover with your fingers. The more holes you cover, the lower the sound. This is because you make the column of vibrating air longer and it vibrates more slowly.

◀ **The trumpet is a wind instrument.**

THE SCIENCE DETECTIVE INVESTIGATES:

Make a Wind Instrument

You will need:
• 3 glass bottles—be very careful when working with glass bottles because if glass bottles smash, the glass can cut you • water

Investigate changing pitch in wind instruments.

1　Fill the first bottle one-third full with water.
2　Fill the second bottle half-full with water.
3　Fill the third bottle two-thirds full with water.
4　Blow across the top of the bottles. Why do the bottles make a sound? Does each bottle sound different?

blow across the top

The bottles make a sound when you blow because the column of air vibrates. The more water is in the bottle, the smaller the column of air, and the higher-pitched the note sounds.

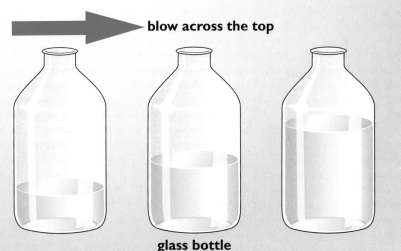

glass bottle

What Is Sound Insulation?

Musicians recording a track do not want any extra noise to spoil the recording. They record their music in a room that does not let any sounds in or out. The room is sound insulated. **Insulation** is material through which sound cannot travel.

Absorbing Sound

Sounds usually seem louder in a big, empty hall at school than they do at home in your living room. Thick carpets, heavy curtains, and soft furniture all help to **absorb** and muffle sounds. Materials used for sound insulation are usually soft or contain air spaces. Air does not carry sound very well. Spongy materials such as foam rubber make good insulators.

▼ **This worker is using a noisy chainsaw. He is wearing ear defenders to insulate his ears from the sound while he cuts down the tree.**

THE SCIENCE DETECTIVE INVESTIGATES:

Stop the Sound

You will need:
- small cardboard box with a lid • alarm clock • 6 egg cartons
- cloth • foam • newspaper • bubble wrap
- yardstick or tape measure

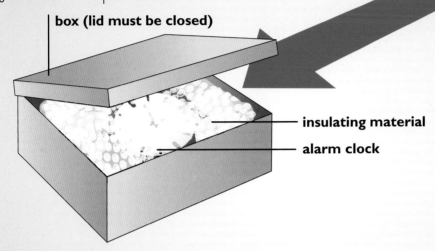

box (lid must be closed)

insulating material

alarm clock

Investigate which materials insulate sound the best.

1 Cut the egg cartons in half, keeping the base of each.
2 Cover the inside walls of your cardboard box with the egg carton bases.
3 Set the alarm clock to go off in 5 minutes.
4 Place the clock in the box and cover it with more egg carton bases and the lid.
5 When the alarm goes off, walk away from the equipment until you can no longer hear the alarm. If your alarm clock is very loud, do the experiment outside.
6 Measure and record your distance from the box.
7 Take out the egg carton bases and replace them with a different material. Repeat the experiment with each test material.
   Which is the best insulator?

Uses of Sound Insulation

Road workers use loud drills to break up the road surface. They may do this for long periods of time, which could damage their hearing. To protect their ears, they wear ear defenders. The ear defenders insulate their ears from the sound.

Sound insulation is sometimes used between two rooms or between two adjoining houses. People do not want to be disturbed by their neighbors.

What Is an Echo?

If you have ever shouted near a cliff or in a very big cave, you have probably heard an **echo**. An echo is a repeated sound. Echoes happen when sound waves bounce off a hard surface and come back toward you.

Hard and Soft Surfaces

When you speak, sound waves move away from you. If they meet a hard surface, the sound waves are **reflected** (bounced off) and come back toward you. If they meet a soft surface, the sound waves are absorbed by the surface. They do not bounce back toward you.

Large Spaces

You can only hear an echo if the hard surface is far enough away. In a small space, it is impossible to hear an echo because it happens at almost exactly the same time as the original sound.

🐾 **Why do you think people do not want echoes to happen in concert halls?**

▼ **When you shout, sound waves move away from you. If they hit a hard surface, they bounce back toward you and you hear an echo.**

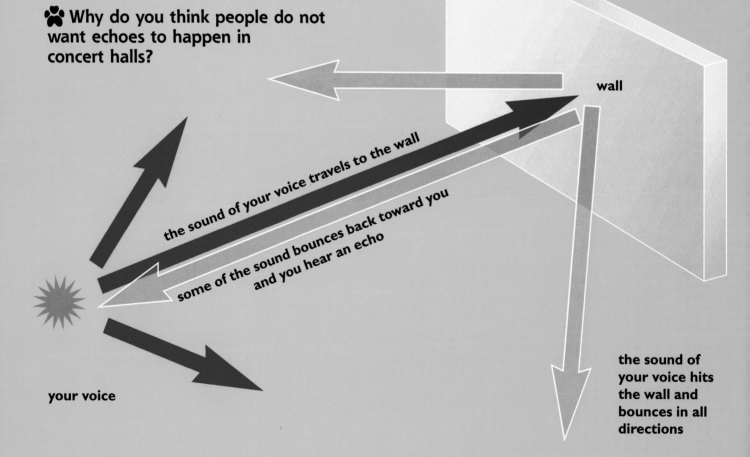

wall

the sound of your voice travels to the wall

some of the sound bounces back toward you and you hear an echo

your voice

the sound of your voice hits the wall and bounces in all directions

THE SCIENCE DETECTIVE INVESTIGATES:

Reflection

You will need:
- strip of cardboard, metal, or plastic
- shallow tray • water • food coloring
- spoon • dropper

1. Arrange the strip of cardboard, metal, or plastic so that it forms a curve at one end of the tray.
2. Fill the tray half full with water.
3. Add a small amount of food coloring.
4. Mix the water until the food coloring has spread out evenly.
5. When the water is completely still, drip one small drop of water into the middle of the tray. Watch carefully. What happens?

The ripples spread out from the drop, hit the curved strip, and bounce back. Sound waves behave in the same way. They spread out from the sound source and bounce back off hard surfaces.

SCIENCE AT WORK

Shouting in a tunnel makes an echolike sound called a **reverberation**. This is not an echo. With an echo, there is a time delay between the original sound and the echo. This happens when the wall surface is more than 56 ft. (17 m) away. With a reverberation, there is no clear time delay between the two sounds. Instead, the two sounds combine and you hear one long sound.

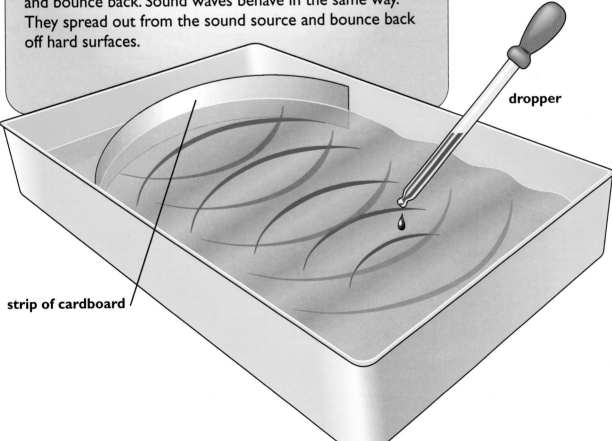

dropper

strip of cardboard

How Is Sound Used?

Sound is used for communication. We use our voices to ask questions and give information, we shout to warn of danger, and cry if we are upset. Sound also tells us about our surroundings. Traffic noise, the sound of the wind, and even our footsteps on the ground give us information. There are also less obvious uses of sound.

Sonar

Explorers and scientists use **sonar** to find underwater objects. A sound signal is sent from a boat into the water. If the sound hits an object, some of the sound reflects back to the boat. This tells the scientists how far away the object is, and in which direction. Very experienced sonar scientists can even use sonar to tell the difference between a large rock, a school of fish, a whale, and a submarine.

▼ This sonar scans the ocean floor from above and from the side. These two types of sonar give scientists on the boat information about the shape and depth of the ocean floor.

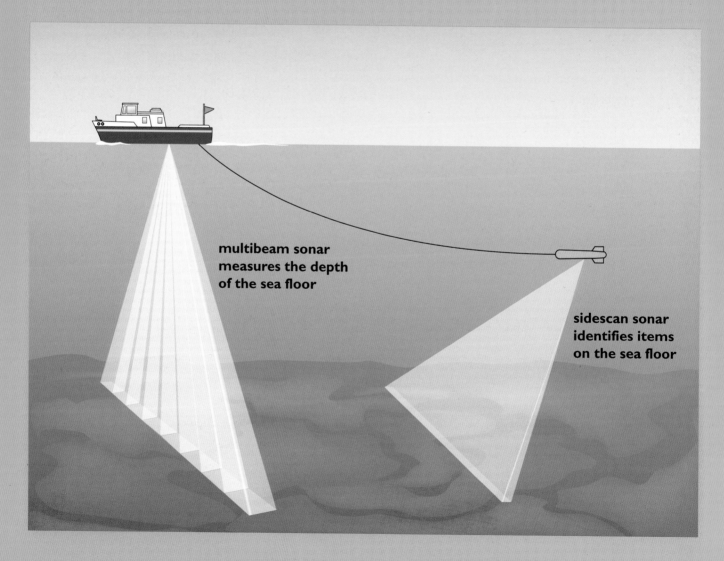

multibeam sonar measures the depth of the sea floor

sidescan sonar identifies items on the sea floor

Echolocation

Animals such as bats, whales, and dolphins use a type of sonar called **echolocation**. Dolphins send out clicking sounds into the ocean. The sounds are reflected by fish and bounce back to the dolphin. The dolphin continues sending out clicks and is able to tell where the fish is, which direction it is traveling, and at what speed. It will then find the fish and eat it. Dolphins' echolocation is so good that they can detect a 1 in. (2.5 cm) object at a distance of 236 ft. (72 m).

▼ **Dolphins listen to their click echoes to create an image of objects in the ocean.**

SCIENCE AT WORK

To find their way around, visually impaired people tap a white stick as they walk. The taps give them information about nearby obstacles. New technology has gone a step farther. The visually impaired person wears a device that includes GPS (global positioning systems), a laptop, cameras, and compasses. To navigate (find their way), the user speaks to the device and tells it where they want to go. Low sounds are played directly to the bones behind the user's ears. The user must turn and walk in the direction of the sounds. Using this technology, the user can find their way to almost any destination.

How Do We Measure Sound?

We often describe sound using words. A dog's bark, the sea gently lapping, and the knock on a door tell us how something sounds. To describe sounds in a scientific way, it is best to measure sound. We can measure the loudness or the **pitch** of sound.

Decibels

The loudness of a sound is measured in units called **decibels** (dB). Humans cannot hear a sound that is 0 dB. Rustling leaves have a loudness of 10 dB, chatting to your friends is around 60 dB, and a food blender is 90 dB.

▼ **The sound at the front row of a rock concert has a loudness of around 110 dB.**

Hearing Damage

Listening to sounds louder than 85 dB for long periods of time can affect your hearing. The sound waves damage tiny hairs inside your inner ear. The hairs cannot repair themselves and hearing suffers. People who work in very noisy environments, such as some factories, airports, rock concerts, and building sites, should protect their hearing by wearing ear defenders or ear plugs.

Hertz

Objects that vibrate quickly make high-pitched sounds and objects that vibrate slowly make low-pitched sounds. To measure the pitch of a sound, a machine calculates how many vibrations take place each second. The unit for this measurement is **hertz** (Hz). Humans cannot usually hear sounds below 20 Hz or above 20,000 Hz. The pitch of normal speech is between 125 and 8,000 Hz.

Type of Animal	Approximate Range (Hz)
Bat	2,000–110,000
Beluga whale	1,000–123,000
Rabbit	360–42,000
Sheep	100–30,000
Dog	67–45,000
Human	64–20,000
Horse	55–33,500
Cat	45–64,000
Cow	23–35,000
Goldfish	20–3,000
Elephant	16–12,000

▲ Elephants can hear extremely low sounds.

🐾 Sound can be so loud that it hurts your ears. This level of sound is called the threshold of pain. At how many decibels does sound become painful? Use the Internet or reference books to find out.

Are there Sounds that Humans Cannot Hear?

Ultrasound is an extremely high-pitched sound. Its pitch is above 20,000 Hz. Humans cannot hear it. Ultrasound waves are used to look inside the human body and to discover what lies beneath the ocean waves. **Infrasound** is an extremely low-pitched sound. Some animals use infrasound to communicate. Scientists are investigating ways to use infrasound to detect **tornadoes**.

Medical Ultrasound

People have ultrasound scans in hospitals. Pregnant women have ultrasound scans to see their babies. The scans are so sensitive they can even show the heartbeat of the baby. The imaging machine sends ultrasound waves into the body. The waves bounce off some types of tissue but travel farther through other types. The machine detects the waves that bounce back to it. It forms an image of the body's internal organs on a screen.

▼ **This is an ultrasound scan of a foetus (an unborn baby). The head is to the right, a hand is touching the head, and the legs are to the left.**

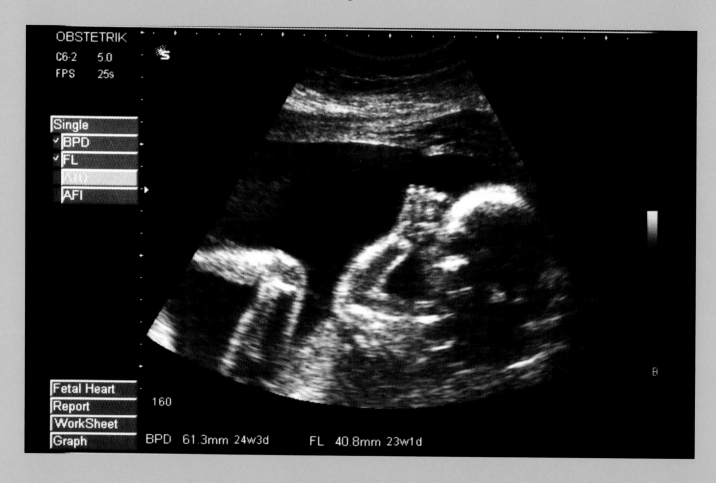

Animals and Ultrasound

Many animals can hear ultrasound. Baby rats make very high-pitched ultrasound squeaks. The sound makes adult rats come to their rescue. A type of Chinese frog that lives in a waterfall makes an ultrasound croak. It does this so that it can be heard above the noise of the rushing water. Dogs can hear ultrasound. Ultrasound dog whistles sound silent to humans, but dogs respond to them.

◀ **A dog comes running to an ultrasound whistle.**

SCIENCE AT WORK

Sounds with a pitch lower than 20 Hz are infrasounds. Infrasound waves have very slow, very big vibrations. In the 1980s, scientists discovered that elephants communicate using infrasound. They use it to attract mates and to coordinate their family groups. Their rumbles can travel from 1.2–2.5 miles (2–4 km). Infrasound vibrations are very large and can sometimes be dangerous. They have been developed into weapons. Their effects include nausea, dizziness, choking, fainting, and even organ damage and death.

Your Project: Which State of Matter Does Sound Travel through Best?

Everything is made of **matter**—you, plants and animals, the ground, and the air. Matter can exist as gas, liquid, or solid. These are the three states of matter. Sound travels through matter, but does the state of matter affect sound travel? Does sound travel more easily through a gas, a liquid, or a solid?

Prediction

Before we investigate how matter affects sound travel, we make a general prediction about what we think might happen. For example, the prediction could be: *Sound will travel more easily through gas.*

Hypothesis

Next, it is important to make a **hypothesis**. A hypothesis is a very specific statement about what you think might happen in your investigation. For this experiment, it could be: *Sound will travel through gas more easily than through liquid or solid.* Use this hypothesis or make up your own one.

You will need
- 3 large plastic bags
- 3 twist ties
- water
- modeling clay or large stone
- table
- someone to help you
- pencil

Method

1 Blow air into a plastic bag. Twist the top of the bag and tie it tightly with a twist tie so that air cannot escape.

2 Fill the second plastic bag with water. It should be approximately as full as the bag filled with air. Twist the top of the bag and tie it with a twist tie.

3 Fill the third plastic bag with one solid piece of modeling clay. Again, it should be filled approximately the same amount as the two other bags. Twist the top of the bag and tie it with a twist tie.

4 Place the air bag on the table and put your ear to it. Block your other ear with your hand.

5 Ask your friend to tap the table with the pencil. Listen to the sound.

6 Repeat steps 4 and 5 with the other two bags. Make sure your friend taps the table with the same force and at the same distance from you each time. With which bag does the sound seem loudest?

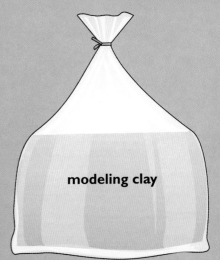

air **water** **modeling clay**

▲ It is important that each bag is the same size and filled to the same level.

What Happened and Why?

The sound should seem loudest with the bag of modeling clay. The tiny particles that make up all matter are closer together in solids than in liquids and gases. The closer together the particles, the more easily sound vibrations can travel through the substance. The sound will seem quietest with the bag of air. The particles that make up air are widely spaced. Were your predictions correct? Did your hypothesis prove to be correct or incorrect? What can you conclude from your investigation?

▼ The particles are tightly packed in a solid (left), slightly spread out in a liquid (center), and very spread out in a gas (right).

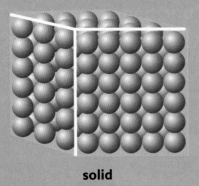
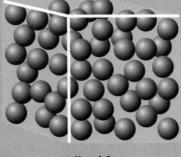
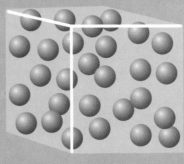

solid **liquid** **gas**

Glossary

absorb To soak up.

amplify To make a sound louder.

asteroid A rocky object in space that can be anywhere from a few yards wide to several miles wide.

communicate To pass on thoughts, messages, and other information.

decibel A measure of the loudness of sound. The unit for decibels is dB.

eardrum A thin membrane inside the ear that vibrates when sound waves hit it.

echo When a sound travels to a hard surface, bounces off it, and returns to its starting point, we hear it as an echo.

echolocation A way in which sound is used to locate (find) an object.

emotions Strong feelings.

energy The ability to do work.

hertz A measure of the pitch of sound—how high or low a sound is. The unit for hertz is Hz.

hypothesis A specific statement about what you think will happen in an investigation.

infrasound Sounds that are very low-pitched, lower than 20 Hz.

insulation A material that stops sound from passing through it.

matter Something that has mass and exists as a solid, liquid, or gas.

music The arrangement of sounds in a way that is pleasant, rhythmic, or makes a tune.

note A sound that has a particular pitch.

percussion Sounds caused by striking two objects together. A drum is a percussion instrument.

pitch How high or low a note sounds.

prey Animals that are hunted and eaten by other animals.

reflect To bounce off.

reverberation When a sound is quickly repeated as a result of it bouncing off a surface.

shock wave A very large, powerful wave that travels away from an explosion.

sonar A system that uses sound waves to detect objects under the sea and the distance to the sea floor.

sound waves The way in which sound travels through solid, liquid, or gas.

streamlined A smooth shape that can easily slip through liquid or gas. Dolphins, sports cars, and airplanes are streamlined.

tornado A column of air that spins very quickly. Tornado winds are very powerful and cause damage wherever they strike.

ultrasound Sound that is too high for humans to ear. Ultrasound has a pitch higher than 20,000 Hz.

vibrate To move back and forth very rapidly.

vocal cords Two thin, skinlike sheets found in the throat. When air passes over the vocal cords, they vibrate and create sound.

Answers

🐾 **Page 4:** Example answer: Sound's vibrations can be felt when a large vehicle, such as a train or a truck, rumbles past, when fireworks or thunder make a loud noise, when you speak or sing, when an instrument is played, and when a speaker emits music.

🐾 **Page 8:** By cupping your hands behind your ears, you are able to catch more sounds. The sound waves are channeled into your ears and everything sounds louder.

🐾 **Page 12:** A bird singing and a child talking are sounds that have a high pitch. A car engine, a lawn mower, and an adult talking are sounds that have a lower pitch.

🐾 **Page 15:** Your vocal cords move closer together to make a high-pitched scream.

To make a low-pitched sound, they move farther apart.

🐾 **Page 19:** The shortest recorded distance represents the best sound insulator.

🐾 **Page 20:** Concert halls are usually large, relatively empty buildings. They create echoes, which interrupt the original sounds. It is harder to hear the notes of the music, if each sound causes an echo. Diffusers are used to avoid echoes. These are specially designed shapes that scatter sound waves in all directions.

🐾 **Page 25:** Sound becomes painful to listen to when it is between 125 and 140 dB. The threshold of pain varies depending on several factors, including age and how often the person is exposed to loud sounds.

Further Reading and Web Sites

Books

All About Light and Sound
by Connie Jankowski
(Compass Point Books, 2010)

Solving Science Mysteries: Why Does Sound Travel?
by Nicholas Brasch
(PowerKids Press, 2010)

The Science of a Rock Concert: Science in Action
by Kathy Allen
(Capstone Press, 2010)

Web Sites

For Web resources related to the subject of this book, go to: http://www.windmillbooks.com/weblinks and select this book's title.

Index

The numbers in **bold** refer to pictures